NICK IS SICK

By Sandy Riggs
Illustrated by Carol Koeller

Table of Contents

Nick Is Sick 4

Fun Facts About Germs and Viruses 20

Activity: A Get-Well Book 22

Word List 24

Illustrations on pages 21–23 created by Carol Stutz

All inquiries should be addressed to:
Barron's Educational Series, Inc.
250 Wireless Boulevard
Hauppauge, New York 11788
www.barronseduc.com

Library of Congress Catalog Card No.: 2005054876

ISBN-13: 978-0-7641-3284-1
ISBN-10: 0-7641-3284-9

Library of Congress Cataloging-in-Publication Data
Riggs, Sandy, 1940–
     Nick is Sick / Sandy Riggs.
          p. cm. – (Reader's clubhouse)
     Summary: While Nick spends the day sick in bed, his friend Bill brings him gifts.
Includes facts about germs and viruses, a related activity, and word list.
          ISBN-13: 978-0-7641-3284-1
          ISBN-10: 0-7641-3284-9
          (1. Sick—Fiction.) I. Title. II. Series.

PZ7.R44247Nic2006
(E)—dc22

2005054876

PRINTED IN CHINA
9 8 7 6 5 4 3 2 1

Dear Parent and Educator,

Welcome to the Barron's Reader's Clubhouse, a series of books that provide a phonics approach to reading.

Phonics is the relationship between letters and sounds. It is a system that teaches children that letters have specific sounds. Level 1 books Introduce the short-vowel sounds. Level 2 books progress to the long-vowel sounds. This progression matches how phonics is taught in many classrooms.

Nick Is Sick introduces the short "i" sound. Simple words with this short-vowel sound are called **decodable words.** The child knows how to sound out these words because he or she has learned the sound they include. This story also contains **high-frequency words.** These are common, everyday words that the child learns to read by sight. High-frequency words help ensure fluency and comprehension. **Challenging words** go a little beyond the reading level. The child will identify these words with help from the illustration on the page. All words are listed by their category on page 24.

Here are some coaching and prompting statements you can use to help a young reader read *Nick Is Sick:*

- **On page 4, "sick" is a decodable word. Point to the word and say:**

  Read this word. How did you know the word? What sounds did it make?

  Note: There are many opportunities to repeat the above instruction throughout the book.

- **On page 8, "ship" is a challenging word. Point to the word and say:**

  Read this word. It rhymes with "hip." How did you know the word? Did you look at the picture? How did it help?

You'll find more coaching ideas on the Reader's Clubhouse Web site: *www.barronsclubhouse.com.* Reader's Clubhouse is designed to teach and reinforce reading skills in a fun way. We hope you enjoy helping children discover their love of reading!

Sincerely,

Nancy Harris

Nancy Harris
Reading Consultant

Nick is sick.

Nick is too sick to
play ball.

I miss my pal, says Nick.

I miss my pal, says Bill.

I have a gift for Nick.
It is a ship.

This is a good gift.

Now can I see Nick?

No. Nick is sick, says Dad.

I have a gift for Nick.
It is a fish.

This is a good gift.

Can I see Nick?

No. Nick is still sick, says Dad.

I have a gift for Nick.

Nick will like this gift.

This is the **best** gift.

Fun Facts About
Germs and Viruses

- There are more than 200 kinds of viruses that can cause the common cold.

- Most adults catch 2 to 4 colds a year. Children might catch twice that many.

- You can't become sick just from being outside in the rain or cold, but you are more likely to get sick in the winter. Viruses thrive in cold weather.

- You pick up all kinds of germs on your hands, even when you don't know it. Washing your hands frequently can prevent the spread of germs and keep you healthy.

- Always cover your mouth when you cough or sneeze. This prevents germs from being passed to others.

A Get-Well Book

Make a get-well book for a sick friend.

You will need:
- 2 sheets of white construction paper
- markers or crayons
- stapler

Note to adult: Staple the papers for children or help them use the stapler.

1. Fold each piece of paper in half.

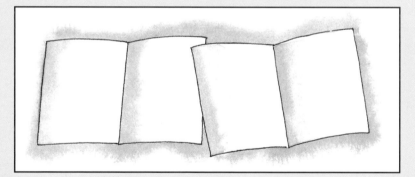

2. Staple the folded papers together to make a book.

3. Write *Get Well* on the cover of the book and decorate it.

4. Draw a picture on each page that will cheer up your friend. You can draw pretty pictures or funny ones.

5. Give this book to your friend.

Word List

Challenging Words	fish ship	
Short I Decodable Words	Bill gift miss Nick sick still	
High-Frequency Words	a can for good have I is it my no now play says	see this